D1096178

AWESOME ATHLETES

ANFERNEE HARDAWAY

Paul Joseph
ABDO & Daughters

visit us at
www.abdopub.com

Published by Abdo & Daughters, 4940 Viking Drive, Suite 622, Edina, Minnesota 55435.
Copyright © 1998 by Abdo Consulting Group, Inc., Pentagon Tower, P.O. Box 36036, Minneapolis, Minnesota 55435 USA. International copyrights reserved in all countries. No part of this book may be reproduced in any form without written permission from the publisher.

Printed in the United States.

Cover and Interior Photo credits: Duomo
                              Allsports

Edited by Kal Gronvall

Library of Congress Cataloging-in-Publication Data

Joseph, Paul, 1970-
   Anfernee Hardaway / by Paul Joseph.
   p. cm. -- (Awesome athletes)
   Includes index.
   Summary: A biography of the Orlando Magic's point-guard superstar whose versatility on the
   court enables his team to be one of the best in the NBA.
   ISBN 1-56239-842-3
   1. Hardaway, Anfernee--Juvenile literature. 2. Basketball players--United States--Biography--
   Juvenile literature. 3. Orlando Magic (Basketball team)--Juvenile literature. [1. Hardaway,
   Anfernee. 2. Basketball players. 3. Afro-Americans--Biography]
   I. Title. II. Series.
   GV884.H24J67   1998
   796.332'092--dc21
   [B]   97-25889
                                                          CIP
                                                          AC

Contents

A True Superstar

Anfernee "Penny" Hardaway is one of the most talented point-guards to ever play in the **National Basketball Association (NBA)**—and he has only played four seasons. He can shoot, pass, block shots, steal the ball, and most importantly, be the team leader.

The six-foot, seven-inch Hardaway is compared to the legendary Magic Johnson. Like the former Los Angeles Laker superstar, Hardaway combines height, ballhandling, a great outside shot, and leadership, into an exciting all-around game. Hardaway has become Orlando's own brand of Magic.

In high school, Penny was an unbelievable player, earning National High School Player of the Year. In **college**, the awards continued to roll in.

Hardaway entered the NBA in 1993, and helped lead his Orlando Magic to the NBA Finals. In 1996, he was a part of the United States Olympic Dream Team. He, along with such stars as Shaquille O'Neal, Scottie Pippen, Grant Hill, and others, dominated the competition and won the gold medal.

Penny worked very hard to become the awesome athlete that he is. He fought the odds, practiced a lot, studied the game, and listened to the advice of his coaches. He also owes a lot to his loving grandmother who was always there for him.

Penny goes in for the slam.

Lil' Penny

Anfernee Deon Hardaway was born on July 18, 1972, in Memphis, Tennessee. His mother's name is Fae Hardaway and his father's name is Eddie Golden. His parents never married and he really never knew his father.

His mother left Anfernee when he was just a baby to start a new life in California. Anfernee, however, still was loved and had a wonderful childhood, thanks to his grandmother.

His grandmother, Louise Hardaway, raised Anfernee from baby to adult. Actually his grandmother gave him his nickname—sort of. As a baby, Anfernee was very pretty. His grandmother would call him "Pretty Baby" or just "Pretty." His grandmother, however, had a very thick Southern accent. So whenever she would say "Pretty" it sounded like "Penny." The nickname stuck and Anfernee has been called Penny ever since.

Penny grew-up in a very rough neighborhood in Memphis. While many of the people in the neighborhood were turning to drugs, gangs, and a life of crime, Penny played basketball and went to school.

His grandmother made sure that he never missed school and was in the house before dark. On Sundays, Penny and his grandmother would never miss church. Every other spare moment was devoted to basketball.

As an eight-year-old, Penny would shoot baskets for up to nine hours a day in the summers and on Saturdays. When it was dark outside Penny would come inside and work on his dribbling and ball-handling. "I never knew a child who liked a basketball more than Penny," said his grandmother.

His classmates in elementary school told him he'd play in the **NBA** some day. Penny didn't believe them nor was it his dream. He played basketball because he loved it and it was an escape from everything else.

High-School Star

Penny attended Treadwell High School. From the first day he walked into the gym as a **freshman**, the coaches knew that he was very talented. He was easily better than kids three and four years older than he was.

Penny led his team to win after win. Because he was one of the taller players on the team, Penny dominated at **center**. Because he was the best ball-handler he would also play point-guard. Whenever the team needed an outside jump-shot they would set up a play for Penny because he had the best shot. He could play any position and guard any player. In fact, Penny would usually guard the best player on the other team.

In his **senior** year in high-school in 1989, Penny put up some unheard of numbers. He averaged 37 points, 10 **rebounds**, 6 assists, 3 steals, and 3 blocked shots per game! For his play he was named National High School Player of the Year.

By now every **college** in the country wanted him. Duke, Georgetown, North Carolina, UCLA, Kansas, Michigan—they all offered him **scholarships**. Everyone knew that Penny would also dominate in college. Even Penny was now thinking about a career in the **NBA**. But before that he had to pick a college.

Penny surprised everyone by choosing Memphis State. Although every college wanted him, Penny chose to stay close to his grandmother. It was a great choice. Penny was happy, his grandmother was happy, and the whole city of Memphis was happy because they would get to continue to watch their hometown hero play basketball.

Penny playing for Memphis State in 1992.

A Very Scary Moment

Although everyone was happy that Penny stayed in Memphis for **college**, that decision almost turned into tragedy. First, Penny couldn't play basketball in his **freshman** year because of poor grades and low college test scores. He was very upset. He knew he let himself down by not studying. Penny was smart enough, but he wasn't working hard enough in school.

Penny didn't play for another reason. As he was walking down the street one day during his freshman year, he was robbed at gun point. As the robber firmly pressed the gun against Penny's neck and demanded his money, Penny prayed he wouldn't be killed. The robber took what little money Penny had and ran away. Then the robber turned as he was running and fired a bullet at Penny. The bullet hit Penny in his right foot and shattered it.

It took Penny many months to get his foot back in shape. He couldn't play basketball for a long time. Penny, however, had a lot of time to think. He thought about his grandmother and what she would have done if he were killed. Penny knew he had talent, and if he worked hard he could make something of himself.

Penny began to study very hard. In his second year of **college** he led his team in grade-point average with a 3.4 and made the Dean's list. His grandmother was more proud of him for that than for any other award he had ever won on the basketball court.

Penny Hardaway at practice during college.

College All-American

Penny worked hard on both his studies and his basketball in his second year of **college**. After getting his foot back in shape, Penny began to shoot, run, and practice basketball. With his studies in order, Penny was ready to lead his team on the court.

Penny came out in his **sophomore** season and dominated the conference in which his Memphis State Tigers played. After the regular season, Penny led the Tigers to the **NCAA** tournament. People all around the country got to see one of the best players in college.

The Tigers fought hard in the NCAA tournament. They won three games and made it to the final eight. There, they were finally beaten. Penny had led them to one game away from the Final Four. For his efforts he was named Great Midwest Conference Player of the Year.

As a **junior** in 1992-93, Penny was even better. He ripped up the Great Midwestern Conference, becoming the first player to be named Conference Player of the Year two years in a row.

For the year, Penny averaged 23 points, 9 **rebounds**, and 6 assists. He set a school single-season **record** for points with 729. Penny again led his Tigers to the **NCAA** tournament where they lost early on.

The loss, however, didn't stop the awards from coming in. Penny was named a First-Team All-American and was a finalist for the Naismith and Wooden Awards (**College** Player of the Year Awards).

Penny directing the Magic offense.

Penny Hardaway is one of the best players in the game today.

1972	1985	1989	1991
Born July 18, in Memphis, TN.	Began playing for Treadwell High School.	Named High School Player of the Year.	Accepted a scholarship to Memphis State University.

How Awesome Is He?

Here is the list of his rookie year statistics and how they compare to other NBA players in their rookie year.

Player	Points Per Game	Total Rebounds
B.J. Armstrong	5.6	102
Clyde Drexler	7.7	235
Anfernee Hardaway	**16.0**	**439**
Kevin Johnson	9.2	191
Mark Price	6.9	117
John Stockton	5.6	105

ANFERNEE HARDAWAY

TEAM: ORLANDO MAGIC
NUMBER: 1
POSITION: GUARD
HEIGHT: 6 FEET, 7 INCHES
WEIGHT: 210 pounds

1992	**1993**	**1993**	**1994**
Named Great Midwest Conference Player of the Year.	Named College All-American.	Drafted No. 3 overall by Golden State then traded to Orlando.	Named to the NBA All-Rookie Team.

- 1989 High School Player of the Year
- 1992 Great Midwest Player of the Year
- 1993 College All-American
- 1994 NBA All-Rookie Team
- Averaged 16 points, 6 Assists, and 5 Rebounds per game in his rookie season with Orlando
- Won a gold medal in the 1996 Olympics.

Highlights

Orlando Finds A Penny

Penny worked hard and became one of the best players in **college** basketball. Everyone knew that he would be a superstar in the **NBA**. He had all of the tools needed to make it. Penny decided that the time was now to try. He left college one year early to join the NBA. Penny knew it was the right time, and he also wanted to give something back to his grandmother.

The Orlando Magic, who already had one superstar on their team, Shaquille O'Neal, won the first pick in the NBA **Draft** Lottery for the second year in a row. With the pick, Orlando chose Michigan's Chris Webber. The Philadelphia 76ers picked Shawn Bradley with the second pick. And with the third pick the Golden State Warriors chose Penny.

However, the Magic really wanted Penny, so they used their number one pick to their advantage by engineering the biggest **draft**-day trade in recent history. The University of Michigan's Chris Webber seemed to be a clear choice as the number one pick. Knowing that Hardaway would probably go third to the Golden State Warriors, the Magic made a trade with them.

The Warriors were thrilled about getting Chris Webber and the Magic were even more thrilled because they got Penny and three future first-round draft choices!

The events of the 1993 **NBA** Draft seemed to assure the Magic of fielding a solid team for years to come. They now had a young and potent inside-outside tandem in O'Neal and Hardaway.

In Hardaway, the Magic got a wonderfully talented point guard whose shooting, passing, and athletic abilities would excite the Orlando fans. The Magic were also looking forward to watching the player who reminded everyone of Magic—Johnson that is. The six-foot, seven-inch Hardaway was looking forward to leading Orlando to the NBA Finals.

A Great Rookie Season

In Penny's **rookie** season in 1993-94, Orlando rose to the top. Not only did they win 50 games and make the **playoffs**, but with Shaq and Penny, the Magic also became one of the top attractions in **professional** sports.

Penny averaged 16 points, 6 assists, and 5 **rebounds** per game in his rookie season. He ranked sixth in the league in steals, was named to the **NBA** All-Rookie First Team, was the only rookie to play in all 82 games, led all rookies in assists and steals, and finished a close second to Chris Webber for the NBA **Rookie of the Year** Award.

With Penny and Shaq leading the way, the Magic reached the **All-Star** break with a 27-20 **record**, and then turned it up a notch, going 23-12 the remainder of the season. They finished in second place in the Atlantic Division and made the playoffs for the first time in team history.

In the **playoffs** the Magic were pitted against the Indiana Pacers. The young Magic squad played hard in the series but eventually fell to the Pacers. Despite the playoff loss it was still a very successful season for Penny and the Magic. Orlando fans were excited about the future of this young team, especially with their new talented point guard.

Penny doing what he does best—creating.

The NBA Finals

When the 1994-95 season started, teams knew that the Magic were for real. They had Penny and Shaq leading the way. The young, talented, and awesome squad was even better than most had thought.

In only Penny's second season in the league, the Orlando Magic posted the best **record** in Orlando history and the best record in the Eastern Conference for the year, winning a whopping 57 games. They easily won the Atlantic Division and advanced to the **playoffs**.

Hardaway evolved into a star himself in only his second season. Kids were wearing his Number 1 Orlando Magic jersey and tried to play like him on the playgrounds. Penny averaged 20 points and 7 assists per game. He started in the **All-Star Game** and earned a spot on the All-**NBA** Second Team.

The Magic raced through the playoffs on their way to an Eastern Conference title. They dominated the Boston Celtics in the first round. They then bounced past the

Michael Jordan led Chicago Bulls. In the Eastern Conference Finals they were matched against the Indiana Pacers. The Magic took them too and advanced to the **NBA** Finals.

Penny was one of the main reasons the Magic made it to the NBA Finals. He averaged over 20 points per game and dished-out 7 assists in the **playoffs**. Penny was very excited to be in the NBA Finals.

In the NBA Finals the Magic took on the Western Conference Champion, Houston Rockets. Penny and Shaq played very well. But in the end the Rockets were too much and swept the Magic in four-straight.

In 1995-96, Penny and the Magic had their best regular season ever. They won 60 games and grabbed the Atlantic Division crown again. Penny played in every game and bumped his scoring average up to nearly 22 points per game. Penny earned his second start in the **All-Star Game**.

After making the playoffs, the Magic strolled through to the Eastern Conference Finals. This time they were matched against the best team in the NBA, the Chicago

Bulls. The Bulls were too much for the Magic and swept the defending Eastern Conference Champions.

Although the season was over for the Orlando Magic, Penny was still playing. However, this time it would be for another team— known simply as the Dream Team.

Penny with the USA Dream Team in the 1996 Olympics.

A Gold Medal

Because Penny is one of the best players in the **NBA**, he was chosen to represent his country in the **Olympics**. The United States Olympic basketball team put together the best team in the world.

Some of the NBA stars that joined Penny were Grant Hill, Charles Barkley, Scottie Pippen, Hakeem Olajuwon, Shaquille O'Neal, and Reggie Miller, to name just a few.

Penny and the "Dream Team" dominated the competition. Other teams were more excited about getting their picture taken with Penny and the rest of the Dream Team than playing the game. Penny said that the entire experience at the Olympics was incredible. When it was all over, Penny and the Dream Team had won a gold medal.

In the 1996-97 season Penny was back playing with the Orlando Magic. However, this year he would be the new leader of the team. Free-agent Shaquille O'Neal left the Magic for the Los Angeles Lakers. Penny was very excited about being the team leader.

Penny continued to prove that he was one of the best players in the **NBA**. He led his team with 20 points per game. Penny was also selected to start in the **All-Star Game**. He also suffered an injury that kept him out of 23 games. However, Penny came back and led his team to 45 wins and a playoff spot.

In the **playoffs** the Magic were matched against their state rival the Miami Heat. The Heat were too much for the Magic and took them in five games, but they weren't

too much for Penny. Penny was the best player in the series. He averaged 31 points and nearly eight **rebounds** per game. In two of the games he scored over 40 points. Penny, however, is a team player and would have much rather won the series than been the best player in the series.

Penny getting ready to shoot a free throw.

Giving Back

Penny is not only a great basketball player, but he is also a great person. He believes in helping others and giving back to those who are less fortunate. He knows that he is very lucky to have gotten out of his rough neighborhood and wants others to have the same chance.

Penny also realizes that he worked hard to make it. He tries to give children a positive message, but mostly he stresses the same thing his grandmother taught him—study hard, practice, go to church, and stay away from drugs and gangs.

His biggest message is that not everyone can be a superstar **athlete**. People must work hard in school and have dreams. Just because he made it in the **NBA** doesn't mean everyone can.

Penny has many **charities** to which he gives. He never forgets what it was like to grow up poor. Penny does his part to help disadvantaged young kids in the

Orlando area. In 1993, he created his own **charity** called Pennies for Pals, which asks fans for their pennies. In Hardaway's **rookie** season, his organization collected 10 million pennies equaling $100,000. He divided the money among four local children's groups.

Penny making his move to the basket.

A Bright Future

Penny is definitely in a league all his own. Many have compared him to Magic Johnson, and others say that he is more like Michael Jordan. Actually Penny is a combination of both and even adds his own skills and special moves.

Penny is known around the world for his incredible basketball talents. Children as well as adults wear his jersey and imitate his shots. Penny also appears on television commercials. One of the most popular commercials is the one with Lil' Penny. Lil' Penny is a small animated character that looks like Penny but acts just the opposite. He throws wild parties, talks a lot, brags a lot, and comes up with a lot of crazy ideas.

Penny has his own line of clothing and his own basketball shoe. Penny is very popular and has made a lot of money from **endorsements**. He is very smart and controls his money wisely. He believes in **charities** and making sure his family is taken care of, especially his loving grandmother.

Penny has had to overcome a lot of obstacles to become the superstar that he is. It started with his parents abandoning him, the rough neighborhood he grew-up in, his poor grades, and almost losing his life to an armed robber. Through it all he worked hard, listened to his grandmother, and became one of the greatest players in the **NBA**.

The best part about Penny is that he is still young. His future is very bright. At only the age of 25, Penny will be playing for many years. He has done nearly everything in life that he has wanted to accomplish. The only thing left is to win an NBA title. Knowing Penny, that shouldn't be too far off.

Opposite page: Penny has a bright future ahead of him.

Glossary

All-Star - A player who is voted by fans as the best player at his position in a given year.

All-Star Game - A game played at the half-way point of the season between the best players from the Eastern and Western conferences.

Athlete - Someone who is physically skilled and talented at sports.

Center - an offensive player who plays in the middle closest to the basket. They are usually the tallest on the team.

Championship - The final basketball game or series, to determine the best team.

Charities - A fund or organization for helping the poor, the sick, and the helpless.

College - The school you go to after high school for higher education to earn a degree.

Draft - An event held where NBA teams choose amateur players to be on their team. After the lottery teams pick, it then goes according to team record with the best team getting the last pick.

Endorsement - Giving your name and image in exchange for money to sell a product.

Freshman - A first year high school or college student.

Junior - A third year high school or college student.

National Basketball Association (NBA) - A professional basketball league in the United States and Canada consisting of the Eastern and Western Conferences.

NCAA - This stands for the National Collegiate Athletic Association, which oversees all athletic competition at the college level.

Olympics - Athletic contests held every four years in a different country. Athletes from many nations compete in them.

Playoffs - Games played by the best teams after the regular season to determine a champion.

Professional - Playing a sport and getting paid for it.

Rebound - getting the ball after a missed shot.

Record - The best it has ever been done in a certain event. Also the count of wins and losses by a team.

Rookie - A first-year player in a sport.

Rookie of the Year - An award given to the best first year player in that particular year.

Scholarship - A money award used to pay for school given to someone for their particular skills.

Senior - a fourth year high school or college student.

Sophomore- A second year high school or college student.

PASS IT ON

Tell Others Something Special About Your Favorite Sports or Athletes

What makes your favorite athlete awesome? Do you think you have a chance to be an Awesome Athlete? Tell us about your favorite plays, tournaments, and anything else that has to do with sports. We want to hear from you!

To get posted on ABDO & Daughters website E-mail us at "sports@abdopub.com"

Index